| | | | | | | | |
|---|---|---|---|---|---|---|---|
| [illegible] | MG | NA | [illegible] | + 2.2 | + 7.9 | NA | NA |
| qGrowth m | LG | NA | 61.49 | + 3.6 | +11.2 | +34.8 | NA |
| qIncome m | LV | 3/2 | 29.89 | + 2.5 | + 6.6 | +12.1 | +19.1 |
| ncISer m | SF | NA | 17.83 | + 3.8 | + 8.4 | + 6.7 | NA |
| ovtInv m | GI | 2/2 | 9.41 | + 1.0 | − 3.2 | + 1.3 | + 5.8 |
| rowInc m | LB | NA | 17.52 | + 3.4 | + 8.0 | +22.3 | NA |
| rowOpp m | LV | NA | 52.13 | + 2.0 | + 4.7 | +18.3 | NA |
| Yield m | HY | 2/3 | 11.66 | + 0.3 | + 6.4 | + 1.0 | + 9.2 |
| [illegible] | SH | NA | 17.85 | + 0.8 | − 1.6 | +14.0 | NA |
| [illegible] | CS | 3/1 | 10.42 | + 0.6 | − 1.0 | + 2.6 | + 5.4 |
| [illegible] | LG | 4/4 | 18.12 | + 3.3 | + 7.2 | +26.7 | +25.8 |
| [illegible] | MG | 3/4 | 15.72 | + 2.5 | +10.3 | [illegible] | +19.3 |
| [illegible] | ML | 3/3 | 12.08 | ... | − 1.6 | [illegible] | + 6.0 |
| [illegible] | SN | 1/3 | 21.71 | + 1.5 | +31.3 | [illegible] | [illegible] |
| [illegible] | FS | 3/3 | 18.60 | + 0.9 | + 8.2 | + 5.8 | [illegible] |
| [illegible] | SG | NA | 16.28 | + 0.9 | +17.9 | NA | NA |
| [illegible] | MU | 2/3 | 10.49 | + 0.8 | + 1.9 | [illegible] | [illegible] |
| [illegible] | SB | 2/4 | 26.87 | + 2.0 | +14.0 | [illegible] | [illegible] |
| [illegible] | ST | NA | 23.92 | + 5.1 | +18.6 | [illegible] | NA |
| [illegible] | SU | NA | 20.07 | + 3.5 | +24.1 | [illegible] | NA |
| **...elity Adv C** (800) 522-7297 | | | | | | | |
| [illegible] | DH | NA | 19.18 | + 2.1 | + 4.4 | [illegible] | [illegible] |
| [illegible]Grow | MG | NA | 10.92 | + 2.2 | + 8.0 | NA | [illegible] |
| Growth m | LG | NA | 62.29 | + 3.6 | +11.2 | [illegible] | [illegible] |
| Income m | LV | NA | 29.91 | + 2.5 | + 6.6 | [illegible] | [illegible] |
| ncISer m | SF | NA | 17.85 | + 3.8 | + 8.4 | + 6.6 | [illegible] |
| rowInc m | LB | NA | 17.52 | + 3.4 | + 8.0 | +22.3 | [illegible] |
| rowOpp m | LV | NA | 52.27 | + 2.0 | + 4.7 | +18.2 | [illegible] |
| Yield m | HY | NA | 11.68 | + 0.3 | + 6.3 | + 1.0 | [illegible] |
| thCare m | SH | NA | 17.86 | + 0.7 | − 1.6 | +14.1 | [illegible] |
| nCap | SG | NA | 16.32 | + 0.9 | +18.0 | NA | [illegible] |
| ech m | ST | NA | 23.97 | + 5.1 | +19.0 | +73.6 | [illegible] |
| **...elity Adv Focus T** (800) 552-7297 | | | | | | | |
| nclSer m | SF | NA | 18.03 | + 3.8 | + 8.6 | + 7.1 | NA |
| ealth m | SH | NA | 18.07 | + 0.8 | − 1.4 | +14.6 | NA |
| atRes m | SN | 1/3 | 22.12 | + 1.6 | +31.6 | +13.7 | + 7.3 |
| ech m | ST | NA | 24.23 | + 5.1 | +18.9 | +74.4 | NA |
| ilGr m | SU | NA | 20.28 | + 3.5 | +24.5 | +40.8 | NA |
| **...elity Adv Inst** (800) 522-7297 | | | | | | | |
| al | DH | 4/4 | 19.36 | + 2.1 | + 5.1 | +11.1 | +17.7 |
| qGrowth | LG | 4/3 | 64.17 | + 3.6 | +11.8 | +36.3 | +27.6 |
| qIncome | LV | 4/3 | 30.25 | + 2.5 | + 7.1 | +13.2 | +20.4 |
| rowInc | LB | NA | 17.68 | + 3.3 | + 8.5 | +23.6 | NA |
| rowOpp | LV | 5/5 | 52.76 | + 2.0 | + 5.3 | +19.5 | +24.3 |
| Yield | HY | 3/3 | 11.46 | + 0.3 | + 6.8 | + 1.8 | +10.1 |
| tBond | CS | 4/3 | 10.44 | + 0.7 | − 0.6 | + 3.6 | + 6.4 |
| dCap | MG | 3/4 | 15.96 | + 2.6 | +10.8 | +16.9 | +20.5 |
| verseas | FS | 4/4 | 18.86 | + 0.9 | + 8.8 | + 6.9 | +12.5 |
| nCap | SG | NA | 16.42 | + 0.9 | +18.5 | NA | NA |
| **...elity Adv T** (800) 522-7297 | | | | | | | |
| al m | DH | 3/4 | 19.29 | + 2.1 | + 4.8 | +10.5 | +17.5 |
| ngMkt m | EB | 1/4 | 8.78 | + 3.8 | +17.0 | − 8.7 | +10.8 |
| gGrow m | LG | 4/3 | 62.92 | + 3.6 | +11.5 | +35.6 | +26.9 |
| Income m | LV | 3/3 | 30.02 | + 2.5 | + 6.8 | +12.6 | +19.7 |
| ovtInv m | GI | 2/2 | 9.42 | + 1.0 | − 2.8 | + 1.9 | + 6.6 |
| owInc m | LB | NA | 17.65 | + 3.3 | + 8.2 | +22.9 | NA |
| owOpp m | LV | 4/4 | 52.73 | + 2.0 | + 6.0 | +18.9 | +23.6 |
| Yield m | HY | 2/3 | 11.71 | + 0.4 | + 6.7 | + 1.7 | + 9.9 |
| Bond m | CS | 3/2 | 10.43 | + 0.7 | − 0.7 | + 3.2 | + 6.1 |
| Muni m | MI | 3/3 | 10.37 | ... | − 1.0 | + 2.0 | + 5.6 |
| rgeCap m | LG | 4/4 | 18.30 | + 3.3 | + 7.5 | +27.4 | +26.6 |
| dCap m | MG | 3/4 | 15.92 | + 2.5 | +10.6 | +16.3 | +19.9 |
| uniInc m | ML | 4/4 | 12.11 | ... | − 1.4 | + 2.1 | + 6.6 |
| verseas m | FS | 3/4 | 19.09 | + 0.8 | + 8.5 | + 6.4 | +12.0 |
| tFixIn m | CS | 4/3 | 9.22 | + 0.4 | + 1.2 | + 4.3 | + 5.8 |
| nCap m | SG | NA | 16.36 | + 0.9 | +18.3 | NA | NA |
| eatInc m | MU | 2/3 | 10.47 | + 0.8 | + 2.2 | + 1.4 | + 8.0 |
| ratOpp m | SB | 2/4 | 27.59 | + 2.0 | +14.3 | +15.6 | +13.7 |
| **...elity Freedom** (800) 544-8888 | | | | | | | |
| 00 | DH | NA | 12.52 | + 1.5 | + 3.6 | +15.5 | NA |
| 10 | DH | NA | 13.80 | + 2.0 | + 6.0 | +15.6 | NA |
| 20 | LB | NA | 14.69 | + 2.4 | + 7.9 | +16.6 | NA |
| 30 | LB | NA | 14.80 | + 2.4 | + 8.8 | [illegible] | NA |
| **...elity Select** (800) 544-8888 | | | | | | | |
| Trans m | MV | 2/3 | 31.79 | + 2.8 | +28.4 | +14.8 | +16.5 |
| otech m | SH | 2/3 | 42.49 | + 4.9 | + 7.1 | +37.3 | +17.9 |
| okInv m | SF | 5/5 | 44.14 | + 3.5 | +15.7 | + 5.1 | +33.8 |
| aSvc m | MG | NA | 14.61 | + 1.7 | +11.0 | −31.6 | NA |
| emical m | MV | 2/1 | 38.21 | + 1.7 | +17.1 | + 0.3 | + 7.1 |
| mputer m | ST | 5/5 | 75.11 | + 5.0 | +16.8 | +91.2 | +42.8 |
| nsumer m | LG | 4/3 | 31.96 | + 2.0 | + 3.6 | +19.9 | +21.8 |
| fAero m | MV | 2/2 | 58.85 | + 2.9 | +11.3 | + 9.4 | +16.9 |
| vCommu m | SC | 4/3 | [illegible] | + 4.0 | +34.2 | [illegible] | [illegible] |
| ectron m | ST | 4/4 | [illegible] | + 3.9 | +29.3 | [illegible] | +42.9 |
| ergy m | SN | 2/5 | [illegible] | + 1.4 | +35.3 | +16.6 | +13.5 |
| ergySvc m | SN | 1/3 | [illegible] | + 0.8 | +57.1 | − 7.9 | [illegible] |
| Svc m | SF | 5/4 | [illegible] | + 3.9 | + 8.4 | + 8.2 | +28.3 |
| odAgri m | LB | [illegible] | [illegible] | + 1.2 | − 7.6 | − 1.4 | [illegible] |
| ld m | SP | [illegible] | 12.26 | − 2.2 | −10.1 | − 4.4 | [illegible] |
| altCar m | SH | 4/5 | [illegible] | + 0.9 | − 5.6 | + 9.8 | [illegible] |
| meFin m | SF | 3/1 | [illegible] | + 1.8 | + 0.2 | −18.2 | +16.0 |
| ustMa m | SN | 1/4 | 24.87 | + 1.9 | +13.8 | [illegible] | + 4.4 |
| ur m | SF | 5/5 | [illegible] | + 3.0 | + 6.9 | [illegible] | +30.1 |
| sure m | LG | 5/5 | [illegible] | [illegible] | +18.1 | +38.9 | +31.2 |
| eDeliv m | SH | 1/2 | 19.71 | − 2.4 | −15.6 | −28.2 | − 0.5 |

| | | | | | | | |
|---|---|---|---|---|---|---|---|
| **Firstar Inst** (800) 228-1024 | | | | | | | |
| BalGrow | DH | 3/2 | 30.83 | + 1.9 | − 2.5 | + 5.5 | +12.5 |
| BalInc | DH | NA | 11.13 | + 1.3 | + 0.5 | + 8.5 | [illegible] |
| BdImmdex | CI | 4/4 | 27.74 | + 1.1 | − 2.2 | + 3.0 | [illegible] |
| EmgGrow | SG | NA | 10.00 | + 1.3 | − 8.4 | − 6.6 | [illegible] |
| EqIndex | LB | 5/4 | 90.85 | + 3.8 | + 9.6 | +23.0 | [illegible] |
| Grow | LG | 3/2 | 38.53 | + 3.7 | + 2.1 | +17.3 | +20.7 |
| GrowInc | LB | 4/4 | 47.24 | + 2.0 | + 2.4 | +11.5 | +23.3 |
| IntBond | CS | 4/3 | 10.19 | + 0.7 | − 0.5 | + 4.1 | + 6.6 |
| IntlEq | FS | 2/1 | 18.21 | + 0.3 | +18.8 | + 4.4 | − 2.2 |
| MicCap | SG | 2/4 | 16.97 | + 0.9 | +14.4 | + 0.7 | +14.0 |
| ShTmBd | CS | 5/4 | 10.20 | + 0.4 | + 1.3 | + 4.9 | + 6.1 |
| SpecGr | MG | 2/2 | 39.86 | + 0.3 | − 7.8 | − 7.9 | + 6.7 |
| TaxExmt | MS | 4/3 | 10.33 | ... | + 6.1 | + 3.5 | + 5.1 |
| **Firstar Ret** (800) 228-1024 | | | | | | | |
| [illegible] | DH | 2/2 | 30.77 | + 1.8 | − 2.7 | + 5.3 | +12.2 |
| [illegible] | CI | 3/3 | 27.72 | + 1.1 | − 2.4 | + 2.7 | + 7.2 |
| [illegible] | LB | 5/4 | 90.69 | + 3.8 | + 9.5 | +22.7 | +28.0 |
| Grow m | LG | 3/2 | 38.10 | + 3.7 | + 2.0 | +17.0 | +20.4 |
| GrowInc m | LB | 4/3 | 47.15 | + 2.0 | + 2.3 | +11.3 | +23.0 |
| [illegible] | CS | 3/3 | 10.19 | + 0.7 | − 0.6 | + 3.9 | + 6.3 |
| [illegible] | CS | 4/4 | 10.19 | + 0.3 | + 1.1 | + 4.6 | + 6.8 |
| [illegible] | MG | 1/2 | 39.36 | + 0.3 | − 7.8 | − 8.1 | + 7.2 |
| [illegible] | MS | 3/3 | 10.32 | ... | ... | + 3.1 | + 4.8 |
| [illegible] | SR | NA | 9.03 | + 1.1 | + 6.1 | − 4.5 | NA |
| **[illegible] Stellar** (800) 677-3863 | | | | | | | |
| [illegible] m | MB | 2/1 | 12.24 | + 2.1 | − 4.0 | + 0.2 | + 9.6 |
| [illegible] m | DH | 3/2 | 12.67 | + 2.0 | + 3.4 | + 5.2 | +11.1 |
| [illegible] | DH | 3/2 | 12.67 | + 2.0 | + 3.5 | + 5.5 | +11.4 |
| [illegible] m | LB | 4/3 | 22.03 | + 3.3 | + 8.0 | +22.8 | +25.0 |
| [illegible] | LB | NA | 22.02 | + 3.3 | + 8.2 | +22.9 | NA |
| [illegible]A f | ML | NA | 10.16 | + 0.1 | − 1.2 | + 2.5 | NA |
| [illegible]A mp | FS | NA | 11.36 | + 1.8 | + 8.3 | + 7.9 | NA |
| RelValA m | LV | 4/5 | 29.55 | + 3.0 | + 8.6 | +16.9 | +25.8 |
| RelValY | LV | NA | 29.57 | + 3.0 | + 8.8 | +17.2 | NA |
| StratInB m | MU | 1/2 | 9.12 | + 0.9 | − 1.3 | − 4.0 | + 4.1 |
| USGovtInA m | CI | 2/2 | 9.60 | + 0.8 | − 2.9 | + 1.5 | + 6.6 |
| **Firsthand** (888) 883-3863 | | | | | | | |
| FirstTech | ST | 3/3 | 51.95 | + 3.1 | +61.1 | +93.9 | +35.0 |
| TechLead | ST | NA | 25.19 | + 7.4 | +40.4 | +107.0 | NA |
| **Flag Inv A** (800) 767-3524 | | | | | | | |
| Commun m | SC | 5/5 | 40.01 | + 4.4 | +21.5 | [illegible] | +48.3 |
| EmgGrow m | SG | 1/3 | 21.52 | − 0.9 | − 6.8 | − 0.5 | + 6.6 |
| EqPart m | LV | 5/5 | 25.98 | + 3.9 | +13.4 | +26.2 | +27.5 |
| MgdMuni m | ML | 2/3 | 10.54 | + 0.2 | − 1.7 | + 1.9 | + 6.2 |
| RealE m | SR | 2/3 | 12.44 | + 0.6 | + 8.9 | − 5.0 | +10.0 |
| ShIntInc m | CS | 3/3 | 10.18 | + 0.7 | − 0.5 | + 3.4 | + 6.3 |
| TotRtUS m | GL | 2/4 | 9.57 | + 1.3 | − 4.6 | + 1.7 | + 7.7 |
| ValBldr m | DH | 4/5 | 24.98 | + 3.3 | +10.0 | +19.4 | +22.9 |
| **Flag Inv B** (800) 767-3524 | | | | | | | |
| Commun m | SC | 5/4 | 39.37 | + 4.3 | +21.1 | +81.9 | +47.2 |
| EqPart m | LV | 5/5 | 25.58 | + 3.9 | +13.0 | +25.2 | +26.5 |
| ValBldr m | DH | 4/5 | 24.94 | + 3.3 | + 9.6 | +18.5 | +22.0 |
| **Flag Inv Inst** (800) 767-3524 | | | | | | | |
| EmGrABCAT | SG | NA | 21.68 | − 0.9 | − 6.6 | NA | NA |
| EqPart | LV | 5/5 | 26.07 | + 3.9 | +13.5 | +26.5 | +27.8 |
| ShIntInc | CS | 4/3 | 10.31 | + 0.7 | − 0.3 | + 3.7 | + 6.5 |
| ValBldr | DH | 5/5 | 25.19 | + 3.2 | +10.1 | +19.7 | +23.2 |
| **Flex-funds** (800) 325-3539 | | | | | | | |
| HighIndGr b | LB | 4/3 | 24.00 | + 3.9 | +13.1 | +23.4 | +23.4 |
| Muir ap | LV | 3/2 | 7.55 | + 2.3 | + 9.9 | +36.4 | +18.6 |
| **Fortis** (800) 800-2638 | | | | | | | |
| AdvAstAlA xm | DH | 3/3 | 18.97 | + 2.4 | + 4.5 | +14.9 | +17.2 |
| AdvAstAlH xm | DH | 3/3 | 18.84 | + 2.3 | + 4.2 | +14.1 | +16.6 |
| AdvCapApA m | MG | 1/1 | 31.71 | + 1.5 | + 8.8 | +20.0 | + 6.8 |
| AdvHiYldA m | HY | 1/2 | 6.76 | + 0.4 | + 1.1 | − 0.8 | + 5.9 |
| AdvHiYldH m | HY | 1/2 | 6.76 | + 0.4 | + 1.1 | − 1.2 | + 5.3 |
| CapitalA m | LG | 3/3 | 23.61 | + 3.1 | + 9.4 | +24.8 | +23.8 |
| CapitalH m | LG | 3/3 | 22.57 | + 3.1 | + 8.9 | +23.8 | +22.9 |
| GlobGroA m | WS | 3/2 | 28.07 | + 2.4 | + 7.8 | + 7.1 | + 9.0 |
| Growth A m | MG | 2/3 | 29.37 | + 2.2 | + 1.4 | + 9.3 | +13.5 |
| Growth H m | MG | 2/3 | 27.96 | + 2.2 | + 1.0 | + 8.5 | +12.7 |
| Growth Z | MG | 2/3 | 29.76 | + 2.2 | + 1.6 | + 9.7 | +13.8 |
| TaxMN E f | SL | 2/3 | 10.14 | + 0.2 | − 1.1 | + 2.5 | + 5.8 |
| TaxNatE f | ML | 2/2 | 10.73 | + 0.2 | − 1.8 | + 1.5 | + 6.0 |
| USGovt A m | GI | 3/3 | 9.05 | + 0.8 | − 2.3 | + 2.3 | + 6.6 |
| USGovt E f | GI | 3/3 | 9.05 | + 0.8 | − 2.2 | + 2.6 | + 6.9 |
| Value A m | LB | 3/2 | 13.94 | + 2.7 | + 8.3 | + 8.6 | +17.4 |
| **Forum** (207) 879-8900 | | | | | | | |
| InvBond f | CI | 3/4 | 10.02 | + 0.9 | − 2.2 | [illegible] | + 6.8 |
| InvEquity f | LG | NA | 13.30 | + 3.3 | + 5.6 | +23.7 | NA |
| InvHiGrBd f | CI | NA | 9.66 | + 1.0 | − 2.6 | + 2.9 | NA |
| MEMuBond f | SI | 3/4 | 10.83 | + 0.1 | − 0.7 | + 2.7 | + 5.7 |
| TaxSvrBd f | MI | 3/4 | 10.87 | + 0.2 | − 0.8 | + 2.2 | + 5.5 |
| **Forward** (800) 999-6809 | | | | | | | |
| Equity | LB | NA | 13.10 | + 3.3 | + 8.4 | NA | NA |
| GlobAstAl | IH | NA | 10.48 | + 1.6 | − 6.6 | − 7.2 | NA |
| GlobBond | IB | NA | 10.06 | + 0.7 | + 0.8 | NA | NA |
| SmCap | SB | NA | 12.15 | + 0.9 | + 6.7 | NA | NA |
| **Founders** (800) 525-2440 | | | | | | | |
| Bal b | DH | 3/3 | 12.18 | + 0.9 | + 0.5 | [illegible] | +13.0 |
| Discover b | SG | 2/3 | 28.22 | + 1.4 | +15.8 | +28.0 | +14.2 |
| Frontier b | MG | 1/2 | 27.30 | + 2.6 | + 7.1 | +10.8 | + 7.2 |

| | | | | | |
|---|---|---|---|---|---|
| **GE Instl** (800) 493-3042 | | | | | |
| Income | CI | NA | 9.66 | + 0.9 | − |
| IntlEq | FS | NA | 12.35 | + 1.1 | + |
| [illegible] | | | [illegible] | + 3.4 | +1 |
| [illegible] | | | [illegible] | + 0.4 | + |
| USCore | | | [illegible] | + 3.3 | + |
| **GMO III** (617) 330-7500 | | | | | |
| CHgIntlBd | IB | 5/5 | 10.69 | + 1.0 | + |
| CHgIntlCr | FS | 4/4 | 10.73 | + 1.1 | +1 |
| DomBd | CI | 3/3 | 9.43 | + 1.2 | − |
| EmgDbt d | EB | 1/3 | 7.69 | + 4.6 | +1 |
| EmgMkt d | EM | 2/3 | 9.38 | + 3.1 | +4 |
| EvCtry | EM | NA | 9.41 | + 4.2 | +5 |
| For | FS | NA | 13.50 | + 0.4 | + |
| GloBal pd | IH | NA | 11.44 | NA | + |
| GloBd | IB | 2/3 | 9.68 | + 0.3 | − |
| GloEq pd | FS | NA | 10.09 | NA | +1 |
| Growth | LG | 5/4 | 4.56 | + 4.1 | +1 |
| IntlBd | IB | 1/2 | 9.84 | − 0.1 | − |
| IntlCore | FS | 3/3 | 22.77 | ... | + |
| [illegible] | FS | NA | 9.84 | NA | +1 |
| [illegible] d | FS | 3/2 | 12.28 | + 0.5 | + |
| [illegible] | [illegible] | 2/2 | 7.58 | − 0.9 | +1 |
| [illegible] | LV | 4/3 | 17.45 | + 2.0 | + |
| [illegible] | SR | 2/2 | 10.17 | + 0.9 | + |
| [illegible] | CS | NA | 9.66 | + 0.1 | + |
| SmCapGr d | SB | NA | 11.91 | + 1.9 | + |
| SmCapVal d | SV | 2/4 | 13.49 | + 1.0 | + |
| [illegible] | LB | 5/4 | 15.61 | + 3.3 | +1 |
| [illegible] | CI | NA | 10.20 | + 0.9 | − |
| [illegible] | CI | NA | 7.11 | + 1.0 | − |
| [illegible] | LV | 5/5 | 20.36 | + 3.3 | + |
| Value | LV | 4/4 | 11.96 | + 2.4 | +1 |
| **GMO IV** (617) 330-7500 | | | | | |
| CHglCr | FS | NA | 10.72 | + 1.1 | +1 |
| EmgDbt | EB | NA | 7.69 | + 4.6 | +1 |
| EmgMkt | EM | NA | 9.37 | + 3.1 | +4 |
| For | FS | NA | 13.50 | + 0.4 | + |
| IntlCore | FS | NA | 22.76 | ... | + |
| USCore | LV | NA | 20.35 | + 3.3 | + |
| **Gabelli** (800) 422-3554 | | | | | |
| ABC b | MG | 3/5 | 10.13 | + 0.4 | + |
| Asset b | MB | 5/5 | 40.40 | + 1.8 | +1 |
| EqIncome b | LV | 4/4 | 18.23 | + 2.5 | + |
| GloInter b | SC | 5/4 | 22.97 | + 1.1 | +3 |
| GloTele b | SC | 5/3 | 21.53 | + 2.3 | +2 |
| Growth b | LG | 5/5 | 39.97 | + 4.6 | +1 |
| SmCapGro b | SB | 3/5 | 22.17 | + 0.7 | + |
| Value m | MB | 5/5 | 19.19 | + 2.2 | +1 |
| **Galaxy Retail** (800) 628-0414 | | | | | |
| AssetAlc f | DH | 3/4 | 17.72 | + 2.0 | + |
| EqGrow f | LG | 4/3 | 28.64 | + 3.8 | +1 |
| EqInc f | LB | 3/2 | 19.78 | + 1.5 | + |
| EqValue f | LV | 4/3 | 20.03 | + 4.4 | + |
| GrowInEq f | LV | 4/4 | 17.43 | + 3.6 | +1 |
| HiQualBd f | CL | 2/3 | 10.41 | + 1.1 | − |
| IILrgCo | LB | 5/4 | 38.62 | + 3.8 | + |
| IISmCo | MB | 2/2 | 16.90 | + 1.1 | + |
| IIUSTrs | GI | 3/3 | 10.27 | + 1.0 | − |
| IIUtil | SU | 3/2 | 15.35 | + 1.5 | + |
| IntGovt f | CI | 3/3 | 9.97 | + 1.0 | − |
| IntlEq f | FS | 4/4 | 19.05 | + 0.4 | + |
| MAMuniBd f | SL | 2/2 | 10.18 | + 0.2 | − |
| NYMuniBd f | MY | 2/3 | 11.03 | + 0.1 | − |
| SmCapVal f | SG | 2/5 | 13.64 | + 1.3 | + |
| SmCoEq f | SG | 1/2 | 14.63 | + 0.7 | − |
| **Galaxy Trust** (800) 628-0414 | | | | | |
| AssetAlc | DH | 4/4 | 17.70 | + 2.0 | + |
| CoreBd | CI | 3/3 | 10.34 | + 0.9 | − |
| EqGrowth | LG | 4/3 | 28.75 | + 3.8 | +1 |
| EqInc | LB | 4/2 | 19.79 | + 1.5 | + |
| EqValue | LV | 4/4 | 20.08 | + 4.4 | + |
| GrowInEq | LV | 4/4 | 17.47 | + 3.6 | +1 |
| HiQualBd | CL | 3/3 | 10.41 | + 1.1 | − |
| IntGovt | CI | 4/4 | 9.97 | + 1.0 | − |
| IntlEq | FS | 4/4 | 19.30 | + 0.4 | + |
| NYMuniBd | MY | 3/3 | 11.08 | + 0.2 | [illegible] |
| ShTmBd | CS | 4/3 | 9.92 | + 0.4 | + |
| SmCapVal | SG | 2/5 | 13.74 | + 1.4 | + |
| SmCoEq | SG | 1/2 | 15.04 | + 0.7 | − |
| TaxEBd | ML | 4/3 | 10.77 | + 0.1 | − |
| **GW&K** (888) 495-5363 | | | | | |
| Equity b | LB | NA | 14.32 | + [illegible] | + |
| GovSec b | GS | NA | 9.90 | − [illegible] | + |
| Gateway b | DH | 3/4 | 22.41 | + [illegible] | + |
| GenSec | LB | [illegible] | 17.91 | + [illegible] | + |
| Gintel | MB | 3/3 | 19.71 | + 2.2 | +21 |
| **Glenmede** (800) 441-7379 | | | | | |
| CoreFixIn | GI | 4/4 | [illegible] | + 0.8 | − |
| EmgMkt d | EM | 2/2 | 8.78 | + 4.0 | +41 |
| InstIntl | FS | 4/4 | 18.15 | + 0.6 | + |

# Kevin O'Malley
# Bud

**Walker & Company** ✸ **New York**

It was the strangest thing that could have happened to Mr. and Mrs. Sweet-William. Their son, Bud, liked dirt. Not just a little bit, either. He'd jump in it, roll in it, and . . . plant things in it. The very proper, very sensible Sweet-Williams were stunned.

It's not as though Bud's parents didn't appreciate nature. It was just so disorderly, and that would never do. They'd clip, spray, and mow the lawn in perfectly straight lines.

The Sweet-Williams were good parents, and at first they encouraged little Bud's interests. They bought him shovels, pails, and the cutest little gardening outfit.

But, they began to laugh nervously when Bud watered the expensive silk flower arrangement and pruned the plastic ficus tree.

Mr. Sweet-William hoped that Bud would just grow out of this phase. But if anything, he grew into it. He tracked dirt into the house, and his room was turning into a jungle of plants. He even started a bug collection.

Mr. Sweet-William read to Bud from a variety of important books on a variety of subjects. Mrs. Sweet-William showed him how to hold a paintbrush the right way and to keep the colors inside the lines. Bud just liked to cut loose.

Soon Bud had taken over the backyard. He put plants in every possible container. He grew sunflowers, petunias, and zinnias, bellflowers, moonflowers, and geraniums. He even collected scraps from the dinner table to use in his compost pile.

"He is a very pleasant boy," said Mr. Sweet-William hopefully.

"The backyard is sort of interesting," said Mrs. Sweet-William bravely.

But they knew they were in trouble. Grandfather Sweet-William had scheduled a visit.

Is that a dinner plate over there?

Grandfather Sweet-William had taught Bud's dad everything he knew about order. He'd never understand Bud's garden. So they made sure that Bud kept his bedroom door closed. And they pulled the curtains over the windows that looked out on Bud's garden.

Grandfather arrived with his usual presents—a classroom organizer for Bud and a bowl of silk flowers for Mrs. Sweet-William.

After unpacking his silk robe and arranging his socks, Grandfather showed Bud how to organize his crayons.

**He insisted on doing the housework.**

Bud was on his best behavior. Grandfather was so
busy, he never went outside. The visit was going smoothly . . .

Until the storm came.

Lightning flashed, thunder crashed, and hail pummeled the house.

That night Bud lay in bed worrying about his garden. He had gotten it to look just the way he wanted. Everything was in order. Now the storm would mess it all up.

Early the next morning Bud raced out of bed before anyone else was up. It was worse than he'd imagined. Bud sat down and began to cry.

Grandfather heard the back door open and came out onto the patio.

"Who made this?"

"I did," said Bud.

"You planted this garden?" Grandfather asked.

"Yes," Bud sobbed. "And now everything's all messed up."

Bud explained about the sunflowers, petunias, and zinnias, bellflowers, moonflowers, and geraniums. About kitchen scraps, compost piles, and how earthworms improve the soil. Grandfather Sweet-William was impressed.

Mr. and Mrs. Sweet-William woke up promptly at 8:00. They heard voices outside. They remembered the storm. They thought about Bud's garden and about what Grandfather would say when he saw it.

"Dad"—Mr. Sweet-William started talking before he got outside—"Dad, let me tell you a little something about this garden and the young man who planted . . ."

Mr. and Mrs. Sweet-William stopped in their tracks. Bud and Grandfather Sweet-William were filthy. Head-to-toe dirty. And both of them were having a time of it.

"Dad?" asked Mr. Sweet-William, "Are you feeling OK?"

"Change is inevitable, Son," laughed Grandfather,

"except from a vending machine."

The whole Sweet-William family pitched in and put Bud's garden back in order. They straightened the sunflowers, petunias, and zinnias.

They tidied the bellflowers, moonflowers, and geraniums. And Grandfather Sweet-William replanted the rosebush.

Later, after the garden was put back in shape and everyone had cleaned up, the Sweet-William family sat down for lunch. "Hard work is easy to take . . ." said Grandfather.

"When you finish with chocolate cake!" said Bud. Everyone laughed. Especially Grandfather.

# For my brother Pat and his lovely family

First published in the United States of America in 2000
by Walker Publishing Company, Inc.

Published simultaneously in Canada by Fitzhenry and Whiteside,
Markham, Ontario L3R 4T8

Library of Congress Cataloging-in-Publication Data

O'Malley, Kevin, 1961–
    Bud / Kevin O'Malley.
        p.   cm
    Summary: The orderly Sweet-Williams are dismayed at their son's
fondness for the messy pastime of gardening.
    ISBN 0-8027-8718-5 (hardcover) — ISBN 0-8027-8719-3 (reinforced)
    [1. Orderliness—Fiction.  2. Parent and child—Fiction.
    3. Gardening—Fiction.  4. Grandfathers—Fiction.
    5. Rhinoceroses—Fiction.]  I. Title.

PZ7.O526 Bu 2000
[E]—dc21                                          99-052869

Book design by Sophie Ye Chin

Printed in Hong Kong
2  4  6  8  10  9  7  5  3  1

| | | | | | |
|---|---|---|---|---|---|
| SR | 3/4 | 13.14 | + 1.0 | + 8.3 | − 1.0 | +11.5 |
| ES | 3/2 | 14.54 | − 0.1 | − 5.5 | −14.0 | + 8.9 |
| EM | 2/4 | 11.51 | + 2.8 | +38.7 | +37.5 | + 0.5 |
| LB | NA | 14.88 | + 3.8 | + 9.2 | +23.1 | NA |
| IB | 5/5 | 10.53 | + 0.2 | + 3.7 | + 7.0 | + 9.4 |
| GI | 3/2 | 10.89 | + 1.1 | + 5.8 | + 2.6 | + 7.1 |
| FS | 2/1 | 8.48 | + 0.6 | +18.1 | + 7.8 | − 4.0 |
| FS | NA | 8.91 | + 0.7 | +16.2 | + 8.4 | NA |
| FS | 3/2 | 12.81 | + 0.4 | + 8.1 | + 5.3 | + 7 |
| FS | 3/2 | 12.33 | + 0.4 | + 8.1 | + 6.9 | |
| FS | 3/2 | 13.44 | + 0.4 | + 8.2 | + 6.9 | |
| FS | NA | 10.88 | + 0.4 | + 8.3 | − 5.8 | |
| | | 11.29 | + 0.4 | +27.6 | +30.5 | −22.2 |
| FS | 3/2 | 17.50 | + 0.5 | + 6.1 | +10.8 | +10.7 |
| PJ | 1/2 | 9.10 | + 2.8 | +48.2 | +54.8 | −10.9 |
| LB | NA | 11.55 | + 1.1 | NA | NA | NA |
| GS | 3/1 | 21.91 | + 0.4 | +21.0 | − 9.2 | + 7.3 |
| SG | 2/3 | 13.72 | + 1.0 | + 6.1 | − 1.7 | + 8.6 |
| SV | 2/3 | 16.37 | + 1.6 | + 7.8 | + 3.8 | + 10.4 |
| SV | 2/3 | 19.32 | + 1.4 | − 7.8 | − 3.9 | +12.3 |
| SB | 1/2 | 11.45 | + 1.6 | + 6.4 | − 1.0 | + 6.2 |
| LV | 4/3 | 22.67 | + 1.7 | +15.6 | +11.8 | +21.6 |
| LV | 4/3 | 21.53 | + 1.7 | +15.5 | +13.7 | +21.4 |
| LV | 4/3 | 21.42 | + 1.7 | +15.6 | +14.0 | +21.7 |
| LB | 5/5 | 39.61 | + 3.6 | + 9.7 | +22.9 | +28.5 |

**-3800**

| | | | | | |
|---|---|---|---|---|---|
| LB | NA | 16.97 | + 2.9 | + 6.8 | +16.7 | NA |
| CI | 4/3 | 10.29 | + 0.9 | − 1.9 | + 2.4 | + 6.8 |
| LB | NA | 12.79 | + 1.0 | − 0.2 | +18.1 | NA |
| SB | 2/4 | 12.76 | + 0.9 | + 7.2 | − 2.1 | +10.8 |
| LV | 3/2 | 16.60 | + 2.3 | +14.6 | + 9.0 | +19.1 |

**Mutual (800) 225-8011**

| | | | | | |
|---|---|---|---|---|---|
| CI | 2/3 | 9.93 | + 0.8 | − 1.4 | + 3.2 | + 6.1 |
| LB | 4/3 | 20.16 | + 4.0 | + 9.7 | +25.0 | +26.0 |
| LB | 4/3 | 24.14 | + 3.3 | + 8.9 | +17.6 | +24.5 |
| LB | 4/3 | 24.03 | + 3.3 | + 8.5 | +16.8 | +23.7 |
| FS | 3/2 | 13.25 | + 0.8 | + 5.1 | + 7.1 | + 9.8 |
| MI | 2/2 | 10.23 | ... | − 1.2 | + 1.8 | + 4.8 |
| SB | 2/3 | 21.20 | + 1.2 | + 0.1 | − 3.4 | + 4.3 |

**279-0279**

| | | | | | |
|---|---|---|---|---|---|
| CV | 4/5 | 26.52 | + 1.6 | +12.6 | +12.1 | +16.5 |
| SF | 5/4 | 31.46 | + 3.4 | + 7.3 | +12.6 | +20.1 |
| LV | NA | 11.08 | + 1.8 | + 8.4 | +13.1 | +21.3 |
| MV | 2/NA | 23.45 | + 2.9 | + 6.8 | + 5.3 | NA |
| LV | 4/5 | 28.41 | + 3.5 | +13.6 | +22.1 | +27.0 |
| SR | 3/4 | 21.52 | + 0.7 | + 4.9 | − 3.4 | + 1.7 |
| MS | 5/5 | 8.89 | + 0.2 | − 0.2 | + 1.8 | + 5.0 |

**279-0279**

| | | | | | |
|---|---|---|---|---|---|
| CV | 4/4 | 26.23 | + 1.6 | +12.1 | +11.3 | +16.0 |
| SF | 5/4 | 30.68 | + 3.3 | + 6.7 | +11.6 | +19.0 |
| MV | 2/NA | 22.53 | + 2.8 | + 6.4 | + 5.2 | NA |
| LV | 4/4 | 27.94 | + 3.5 | +13.1 | +21.1 | +26.0 |
| SR | 3/3 | 21.41 | + 0.7 | + 4.4 | − 4.4 | + 1.8 |
| MS | 5/5 | 8.86 | + 0.2 | − 0.2 | + 1.1 | + 5.0 |

**279-0279**

| | | | | | |
|---|---|---|---|---|---|
| CV | NA | 26.62 | + 1.6 | +12.7 | +12.6 | NA |
| LV | 4/4 | 28.07 | + 3.5 | +13.1 | +21.1 | +26.1 |
| LV | NA | 28.68 | + 3.5 | +13.7 | +22.5 | NA |
| SR | NA | 21.57 | + 0.7 | + 4.5 | − 4.2 | NA |
| SR | NA | 21.67 | + 0.7 | + 5.1 | − 3.0 | NA |
| MS | NA | 8.92 | + 0.2 | − 0.1 | + 1.8 | NA |
| SV | 2/3 | 14.85 | + 0.3 | +13.7 | − 2.0 | +10.0 |

**523-4640**

| | | | | | |
|---|---|---|---|---|---|
| MG | 5/5 | 27.03 | + 2.8 | +18.3 | +42.8 | +38.6 |
| DH | 3/4 | 23.30 | + 0.9 | − 1.5 | + 9.1 | +16.6 |
| MG | 2/3 | 25.73 | + 1.4 | + 8.6 | +18.9 | +12.9 |
| HY | 3/3 | 5.62 | | + 0.2 | − 6.5 | + 7.0 |
| LB | 4/3 | 21.76 | + 0.9 | − 1.6 | +10.9 | +23.1 |
| LV | 3/3 | 19.07 | + 1.8 | + 5.3 | + 6.8 | +19.0 |
| LV | 3/3 | 18.10 | + 2.1 | + 6.3 | + 3.1 | +20.0 |
| LB | 3/2 | 33.87 | + 2.3 | + 6.3 | +14.5 | +19.2 |
| FS | 3/3 | 16.52 | + 0.1 | + 7.8 | − 1.7 | +10.6 |
| GS | 3/3 | 9.45 | + 0.2 | ... | − 4.9 | + 5.3 |
| SL | 5/5 | 10.48 | + 0.2 | ... | − 3.1 | + 8.3 |
| MI | 5/5 | 10.61 | + 0.1 | + 0.6 | − 4.1 | + 7.9 |
| SV | 2/4 | 26.59 | + 0.4 | + 1.5 | − 0.7 | +13.1 |
| LB | NA | 12.43 | + 2.6 | + 1.9 | + 6.5 | NA |
| MI | 2/3 | 10.61 | + 0.2 | − 1.3 | + 1.3 | + 5.4 |
| SI | 3/1 | 10.7 | + 0.3 | − 0.6 | + 1.8 | + 5.8 |
| MI | 3/3 | 11.17 | + 0.2 | − 2.3 | + 0.1 | + 4.9 |
| SG | 3/4 | 18.35 | + 1.1 | +12.6 | +23.6 | +13.7 |
| CI | 2/2 | 7.37 | + 0.2 | − 2.6 | + 1.0 | + 6.1 |

**523-4640**

| | | | | | |
|---|---|---|---|---|---|
| MG | 5/5 | 26.04 | + 2.8 | +17.9 | +41.7 | +37.2 |
| DH | 3/4 | 23.26 | + 0.9 | − 1.8 | + 8.3 | +15.7 |
| HY | 2/3 | 5.62 | − 0.1 | − 0.1 | − 7.0 | + 6.2 |
| LB | 4/3 | 21.59 | + 0.9 | − 1.9 | +10.1 | +22.2 |
| LV | 3/3 | 18.71 | + 1.7 | + 4.9 | + 5.9 | +18.0 |
| LV | 3/3 | 18.04 | + 2.1 | + 5.9 | + 7.3 | +19.2 |
| FS | 3/3 | 16.47 | + 0.1 | + 7.5 | − 5.4 | + 9.9 |
| SV | 2/3 | 26.65 | + 0.4 | + 1.1 | − 1.4 | +12.3 |
| LB | 3/2 | 12.22 | + 2.7 | + 1.6 | + 5.7 | NA |
| LB | NA | 11.69 | + 0.9 | − 3.0 | + 8.6 | NA |
| SI | 2/2 | 8.07 | + 0.3 | − 1.0 | + 1.0 | + 4.9 |

| MuniBd A f | ML | 3/4 | 13.90 | + 0.1 | − 1.7 | + 0.2 | + 6.3 |
|---|---|---|---|---|---|---|---|
| MuniBd B m | ML | 3/3 | 13.91 | + 0.1 | − 1.8 | − 0.3 | + 5.8 |
| MuniCT A f | SL | 4/4 | 11.95 | + 0.2 | − 0.8 | + 2.9 | + 6.9 |
| MuniCT B m | SL | 3/3 | 11.94 | + 0.1 | − 1.1 | + 2.3 | + 6.3 |
| MuniFL A f | SL | 1/1 | 13.77 | + 0.3 | − 0.8 | + 1.7 | + 5.1 |
| MuniMA A f | SI | 3/4 | 11.37 | + 0.3 | − 1.0 | + 2.0 | + 6.6 |
| MuniMD A f | SL | 4/5 | 12.69 | + 0.3 | − 0.3 | + 2.7 | + 6.8 |
| MuniMD B m | SL | 4/4 | 12.69 | + 0.3 | − 0.6 | + 2.2 | + 6.2 |
| MuniMI A f | SL | 3/4 | 15.19 | + 0.3 | − 0.9 | + 1.9 | + 6.4 |
| MuniMN A f | SI | 3/4 | 14.93 | + 0.2 | − 0.9 | + 2.0 | + 5.6 |
| MuniNC A f | SL | 3/3 | 13.58 | + 0.2 | − 1.1 | + 1.7 | + 7.0 |
| MuniNC B m | SL | 3/3 | 13.57 | + 0.1 | − 1.3 | + 1.2 | + 6.5 |
| MuniOH A f | SL | 3/3 | 12.49 | + 0.2 | − 0.7 | + 2.2 | + 6.3 |
| MuniOH B m | SL | 3/3 | 12.50 | + 0.2 | − 1.0 | + 1.7 | + 5.7 |
| MuniPA A f | SL | 4/4 | 16.17 | + 0.3 | − 0.7 | + 2.6 | + 7.0 |
| MuniPA B m | SL | 3/3 | 16.17 | + 0.2 | − 0.9 | + 2.0 | + 6.4 |
| MuniX A f | SL | 4/4 | 20.85 | + 0.3 | − 1.1 | + 1.9 | + 7.2 |
| MuniVA A f | SL | 3/4 | 16.91 | + 0.2 | − 0.7 | + 2.2 | + 7.3 |
| MuniVA B m | SL | 3/3 | 16.91 | + 0.2 | − 0.9 | + 1.7 | + 6.7 |
| NYMuni A f | MY | 2/3 | 14.78 | + 0.3 | − 1.4 | + 2.1 | + 7.0 |
| NYMuni B m | MY | 2/2 | 14.78 | + 0.3 | − 1.7 | + 1.6 | + 6.4 |
| PreTechGA f | ST | NA | 30.14 | + 3.7 | +46.7 | +125.4 | NA |
| SmCoStkR | MB | 3/1 | 15.05 | + 0.6 | + 0.1 | − 4.8 | + 7.8 |
| TaxMgdGrA m | LG | NA | 17.02 | + 2.3 | + 3.5 | +14.3 | NA |
| TaxMgdGrB m | LG | NA | 16.83 | + 2.2 | + 3.2 | +13.4 | NA |
| TaxMgdGrC m | LG | NA | 16.82 | + 2.2 | + 3.2 | +13.4 | NA |
| Value A f | LV | 2/1 | 22.97 | + 4.2 | + 8.3 | +13.0 | +15.4 |
| Value B m | LV | 2/1 | 22.21 | + 4.2 | + 8.0 | +12.1 | +14.6 |
| WldwdeGrA f | LG | 4/3 | 34.11 | + 1.8 | + 3.5 | +10.6 | +21.1 |
| WldwdeGrB m | LG | 4/3 | 33.21 | + 1.8 | + 3.2 | + 9.8 | +23.3 |
| WldwdeGrC m | LG | 4/3 | 32.92 | + 1.8 | + 3.2 | + 9.8 | +23.3 |

| Driehaus | FS | NA | 12.87 | + 2.3 | +11.4 | − 3.7 | NA |
|---|---|---|---|---|---|---|---|

**Dupree (800) 866-0614**

| KYTxFInc | SI | 5/5 | 7.55 | + 0.1 | + 0.1 | + 3.6 | + 6.5 |
|---|---|---|---|---|---|---|---|
| KYTxFShM | MS | 5/5 | 5.24 | + 0.3 | + 0.3 | + 3.3 | + 4.5 |
| TNTxFInc | SL | 5/5 | 10.91 | + 0.1 | + 0.4 | + 4.2 | + 8.1 |

| EltRealls | SR | NA | 9.58 | + 0.8 | + 6.8 | NA | NA |
|---|---|---|---|---|---|---|---|
| EGCSmCapA m | SB | 1/2 | 18.67 | + 0.9 | + 5.4 | − 4.3 | + 5.8 |
| EaseIIGr b | LG | 2/1 | 15.39 | + 3.8 | − 1.1 | +10.8 | +16.9 |

**Eaton Vance A (800) 225-6265**

| Balanced f | DH | 3/3 | 8.13 | + 2.1 | + 2.8 | + 6.7 | +15.6 |
|---|---|---|---|---|---|---|---|
| CapExch | LG | 5/4 | 514.30 | + 2.8 | + 6.7 | +18.9 | +26.3 |
| FLLtdMu m | SI | NA | 10.02 | + 0.1 | − 1.3 | + 1.7 | NA |
| GovObl m | GS | 3/2 | 10.01 | + 0.4 | − 0.3 | + 3.3 | + 5.9 |
| GrInc f | LB | 4/3 | 16.85 | + 1.6 | + 6.4 | +16.4 | +24.1 |
| GwthIn f | LG | 3/2 | 10.69 | + 3.2 | + 5.1 | +10.5 | +19.8 |
| GrChina m | PJ | 1/3 | 11.12 | + 3.9 | +25.9 | +29.9 | − 7.3 |
| HiIncome m | ML | 5/5 | 10.97 | + 0.2 | − 0.6 | + 0.1 | + 8.7 |
| HiYield m | HY | 4/5 | 8.38 | − 0.2 | + 7.3 | + 4.0 | +11.8 |
| InfoAge m | SR | NA | 10.07 | + 0.8 | − 1.2 | + 2.0 | NA |
| MuniBd m | ML | NA | 9.53 | + 0.4 | − 2.3 | + 1.5 | NA |
| MuniBd f | ML | 5/5 | 10.39 | + 0.5 | − 2.3 | + 1.4 | + 8.4 |
| NJLtdMat m | SI | NA | NA | NA | NA | NA | NA |
| NYLtdMat m | MN | NA | NA | NA | NA | NA | NA |
| NatlMuni f | ML | 5/5 | 10.94 | + 0.3 | − 2.2 | + 0.3 | + 8.0 |
| PALtdMu m | SI | NA | 10.27 | + 0.1 | − 0.6 | + 1.8 | NA |
| SpecEq f | MG | 2/3 | 7.49 | + 1.6 | + 2.5 | +11.8 | +14.5 |
| TaxMgdEGr m | SG | NA | 11.49 | + 1.4 | + 2.8 | +11.6 | NA |
| TaxMgdGr f | LG | 4/4 | 20.73 | + 2.8 | + 5.6 | +18.7 | +26.2 |
| Util f | SU | 3/3 | 11.25 | + 1.4 | +12.9 | +24.5 | +19.4 |
| WldwHeal m | SH | 2/3 | 16.37 | + 1.4 | − 6.4 | +15.7 | + 9.2 |

**Eaton Vance B (800) 225-6265**

| ALMunis m | SL | 2/2 | 10.67 | + 0.4 | − 1.1 | + 1.5 | + 5.4 |
|---|---|---|---|---|---|---|---|
| ARMunis m | SL | 3/3 | 10.46 | + 0.2 | − 0.9 | + 1.8 | + 5.5 |
| AZMunis m | SL | 3/3 | 11.05 | + 0.2 | − 1.2 | + 1.3 | + 6.2 |
| Balanced m | DH | 3/3 | 13.78 | + 2.1 | + 2.8 | + 6.1 | +14.6 |
| CAMunis m | MC | 3/3 | 10.90 | + 0.4 | − 1.7 | + 1.6 | + 6.7 |
| COMunis m | SL | 3/3 | 10.50 | + 0.3 | − 1.4 | + 1.1 | + 6.2 |
| CTMunis m | SL | 3/3 | 10.48 | + 0.2 | − 0.3 | + 2.5 | + 6.1 |
| FLMunis m | SL | 1/1 | 10.92 | + 0.3 | − 1.3 | + 1.2 | + 5.7 |
| GAMunis m | SL | 2/1 | 9.92 | + 0.2 | − 2.2 | + 0.4 | + 5.3 |
| GovObl m | GS | 2/1 | 8.61 | + 0.6 | − 0.1 | + 2.6 | + 5.2 |
| GrInc m | LB | 4/3 | 16.87 | + 1.6 | + 6.1 | +15.5 | +22.9 |
| GrChina m | PJ | 1/3 | 10.01 | + 3.8 | +25.6 | +29.2 | − 7.8 |
| HiIncome m | HY | 4/5 | 7.43 | − 0.3 | + 6.7 | − 2.8 | +10.9 |
| HiYldMu m | ML | 5/5 | 10.92 | + 0.2 | − 1.0 | − 0.7 | + 8.0 |
| InfoAge m | WS | NA | 16.94 | + 2.5 | +18.5 | +26.6 | +20.9 |
| KYMunis m | SL | 3/3 | 10.37 | + 0.4 | − 0.2 | + 3.2 | + 6.0 |
| LAMunis m | SL | 3/3 | 10.10 | + 0.5 | − 2.1 | + 0.5 | + 5.5 |
| MAMunis m | SL | 2/2 | 10.57 | + 0.3 | − 1.6 | + 1.4 | + 6.0 |
| MDMunis m | SL | 1/1 | 10.39 | + 0.3 | − 1.5 | − 0.3 | + 6.1 |
| MIMunis m | SL | 2/1 | 10.81 | + 0.3 | − 1.4 | + 0.7 | + 5.5 |
| MNMunis m | SL | 2/2 | 10.27 | + 0.1 | − 1.6 | + 1.3 | + 5.5 |
| MOMunis m | SL | 3/3 | 10.98 | + 0.3 | − 1.4 | + 1.4 | + 6.2 |
| NCMunis m | SL | 3/3 | 10.25 | + 0.3 | − 1.3 | + 1.6 | + 5.7 |
| NJMunis m | SL | 3/3 | 10.71 | + 0.3 | − 1.3 | + 0.8 | + 6.0 |
| NYMunis m | MY | 2/2 | 11.04 | + 0.2 | − 1.9 | + 1.2 | + 6.1 |
| NatlMuni m | ML | 4/4 | 10.21 | + 0.3 | − 2.5 | − 0.3 | + 6.4 |
| OHMunis m | SL | 3/3 | 10.72 | + 0.3 | − 0.8 | + 1.8 | + 5.9 |
| ORMunis m | SL | 3/3 | 10.53 | + 0.3 | − 0.7 | + 2.4 | + 5.5 |
| PAMunis m | SL | 2/1 | 10.41 | + 0.3 | − 0.7 | + 0.7 | + 5.5 |
| RIMunis m | SL | 2/1 | 9.71 | + 0.4 | − 1.5 | + 1.3 | + 5.9 |
| SCMunis m | SL | 3/3 | 10.17 | + 0.3 | − 2.7 | − 0.2 | + 5.3 |
| StratInc m p | MU | 3/4 | 8.00 | + 1.0 | + 2.4 | − 2.3 | + 8.4 |
| TNMunis m | SL | 3/3 | 10.54 | + 0.1 | − 0.7 | + 2.0 | + 6.0 |

| TotRetls | CI | NA | 93.82 | + 0.5 | − 2.0 | + 0.5 |
|---|---|---|---|---|---|---|

**Excelsior (800) 446-1012**

| BlendEqA | LB | 4/3 | 42.96 | + 3.9 | + 7.3 | +19.0 | |
|---|---|---|---|---|---|---|---|
| CATaxEInc | SI | NA | 7.14 | ... | + 0.1 | − 3.2 | |
| EnerNatRs | SN | 2/5 | 13.29 | + 0.6 | +29.6 | −13.1 | |
| IncGrow | MG | 2/4 | 13.81 | + 0.9 | + 8.7 | + 7.7 | |
| IntTmMgd | CI | 3/3 | 6.93 | + 0.7 | − 2.8 | + 2.7 | |
| Intl | FS | 3/3 | 13.56 | + 1.7 | + 8.8 | − 3.2 | |
| LrgCapGr | LG | 3/3 | 13.87 | + 4.5 | +16.9 | +55.0 | |
| MgdInc | CL | 3/3 | 8.74 | + 0.6 | − 2.6 | + 2.0 | |
| PacAsia | DP | 2/4 | 8.23 | + 2.1 | +34.7 | +63.6 | |
| PanEuro | ES | 4/3 | 12.47 | + 0.7 | − 2.0 | − 3.6 | |
| RealE | SR | NA | 6.06 | + 0.7 | + 5.2 | − 1.2 | |
| ShTmGovt | GS | 4/3 | 6.97 | + 0.2 | + 0.5 | + 4.3 | |
| ShTmTaxE | MS | 4/3 | 7.10 | | + 0.7 | + 3.7 | |
| SmCap A | SG | 1/2 | 10.06 | − 0.5 | + 4.1 | − 7.2 | |
| TaxEInt | MI | 3/3 | 9.23 | − 0.1 | − 1.4 | + 2.5 | |
| TxELgTm | ML | 3/3 | 9.56 | + 0.4 | − 2.1 | + 1.8 | |
| TxENYInt | MN | 3/3 | 8.58 | + 0.1 | − 1.4 | + 2.5 | |
| ValRestA | LV | 4/4 | 26.77 | + 3.8 | +18.0 | +19.6 | |

**Excelsior Inst (800) 446-1012**

| Eq | LG | 5/4 | 14.94 | + 3.7 | +10.3 | +19.3 |
|---|---|---|---|---|---|---|
| Income | CL | 4/4 | 6.79 | + 0.4 | − 2.7 | + 2.2 |
| IntlEq | FS | 3/2 | 9.20 | + 1.5 | + 4.0 | − 3.1 |
| OptGrow | LG | 5/5 | 26.29 | + 4.5 | +15.2 | +54.3 |
| TotalRet | CL | 3/3 | 7.10 | + 0.7 | − 3.7 | + 1.6 |
| ValueEq | LB | 5/4 | 17.00 | + 3.1 | +13.0 | +22.3 |

**Executive Investors (800) 423-4026**

| HighYld m | HY | 2/3 | 7.28 | − 0.7 | + 1.5 | − 1.3 |
|---|---|---|---|---|---|---|
| InsTaxE m | ML | 3/3 | 14.09 | ... | − 1.5 | + 3.1 |

**Exeter (800) 466-3863**

| BldAsstIA | DH | 3/2 | 13.41 | + 2.4 | +10.4 | +12.2 |
|---|---|---|---|---|---|---|
| BlendAstA | DH | 3/2 | 11.49 | + 1.5 | + 4.8 | + 9.9 |

**Expedition (800) 922-2085**

| Bond Is | CS | NA | 9.73 | + 0.7 | − 1.5 | + 3.2 |
|---|---|---|---|---|---|---|
| EquityIs | LB | NA | 12.86 | + 4.0 | +12.2 | +25.4 |
| PAMValue | SV | 3 | 34.55 | + 0.3 | − 0.3 | − 0.7 |

**FBR Contrarian (800) 543-0407**

| Balanced | DH | 4/4 | 20.88 | + 3.0 | +11.0 | +18.5 |
|---|---|---|---|---|---|---|
| Equity | LV | 4/4 | 25.37 | + 3.7 | +15.2 | +24.2 |

**FBR (888) 888-0025**

| FinclSvA m | SF | NA | 16.58 | + 2.5 | − 0.2 | − 5.2 |
|---|---|---|---|---|---|---|
| SmCapFinA m | SF | NA | 14.41 | + 0.4 | + 1.3 | −14.3 |

**FFTW (800) 762-4848**

| Intl | IB | 1/2 | 8.79 | − 0.7 | − 7.5 | + 6.3 |
|---|---|---|---|---|---|---|
| Liquour | GS | 5/5 | 9.77 | + 0.3 | + 0.8 | + 4.8 |
| USShTmFI | UB | 5/2 | 9.69 | + 0.1 | + 1.7 | + 4.6 |
| WldFixI | IB | 2/3 | 9.45 | − 0.6 | − 6.1 | + 4.8 |
| WldFixIH | IB | 5/5 | 10.94 | + 0.7 | − 0.2 | + 6.5 |
| FMIFocus | SB | NA | 21.67 | + 2.4 | +12.5 | +41.6 |

**FPA (800) 982-4372**

| Capital f | MV | 2/2 | 34.95 | + 1.3 | +12.6 | + 3.1 |
|---|---|---|---|---|---|---|
| NewInc f | CI | 4/5 | 10.89 | + 0.1 | + 3.0 | + 3.9 |
| Paramoun f | MV | 1/1 | 8.66 | − 0.2 | − 4.9 | −29.7 |
| Perennia f | MB | 3/3 | 22.42 | + 2.4 | +11.3 | +10.1 |

**FTI (888) 343-8242**

| Bond b | CI | NA | 9.63 | + 0.8 | − 1.0 | NA |
|---|---|---|---|---|---|---|
| IntlEq b | FS | 4/3 | 14.69 | + 1.1 | + 4.8 | − 1.2 |
| LrgCapGl xb | LB | NA | 11.07 | + 3.0 | + 3.7 | NA |
| MuniBond b | MI | NA | 9.69 | ... | − 1.2 | NA |
| SmCapEq b | SG | 3/4 | 15.95 | + 1.9 | + 9.2 | +11.4 |

**Fairport (800) 332-6459**

| GrowInc b | MB | 3/3 | 17.25 | + 3.1 | + 3.7 | + 7.6 |
|---|---|---|---|---|---|---|
| MWGrowth b | MB | 2/1 | 13.28 | + 3.4 | −12.7 | −16.7 |
| Fasciano | SG | 2/5 | 31.42 | + 0.7 | + 0.7 | − 2.7 |

**Federated A (800) 341-7400**

| Bond m | CI | 3/3 | 9.44 | + 1.0 | − 1.3 | + 0.5 |
|---|---|---|---|---|---|---|
| EmgMkt m | EM | 2/5 | 11.35 | + 1.5 | +33.4 | + 6.9 |
| EqInc f | LB | 3/3 | 20.59 | + 3.0 | + 8.8 | +17.5 |
| EuroGrow m | ES | 4/3 | 15.57 | + 0.5 | − 0.4 | − 0.7 |
| GovInSec m | GI | NA | 8.59 | + 1.2 | − 1.9 | + 2.4 |
| GrowStr f | MG | 3/4 | 34.15 | + 3.9 | +18.5 | +26.6 |
| HiIncBd f | HY | 3/4 | 10.99 | + 0.1 | + 2.7 | + 1.5 |
| IntlEq f | FS | 3/3 | 20.44 | + 0.2 | + 4.8 | + 2.7 |
| IntlInc m | IB | 1/2 | 10.24 | − 0.4 | − 7.9 | + 2.8 |
| IntlSmCo m | FS | 5/5 | 23.18 | + 2.2 | +27.7 | +20.7 |
| LtdTrm m | CS | 4/4 | 9.69 | + 0.4 | + 1.3 | + 3.1 |
| LtdTmMu m | MS | 3/2 | 9.72 | + 0.1 | + 0.3 | + 3.0 |
| MInthMu f | SI | 3/4 | 10.75 | + 0.1 | − 1.0 | + 2.3 |
| MuniOpp m | ML | NA | 10.30 | + 0.2 | − 1.7 | + 1.2 |
| MuniSecs f | ML | 1/2 | 10.37 | + 0.2 | − 1.3 | + 1.6 |
| PAMuInc m | SL | 3/4 | 11.53 | + 0.3 | − 1.1 | + 2.0 |
| SmallCap m | SB | 1/2 | 7.61 | + 0.9 | − 2.9 | − 1.1 |
| StratInc xf | MU | 4/5 | 8.29 | + 1.2 | + 1.7 | + 1.3 |
| USGovSec f | GI | 3/4 | 7.66 | + 0.8 | − 2.3 | + 3.3 |
| Utility f | SU | 3/3 | 12.94 | + 2.0 | + 4.5 | +13.6 |
| WldUtil f | SU | 4/4 | 11.77 | + 2.7 | +11.9 | +24.2 |

**Federated B (800) 341-7400**

| Bond m | CI | 2/2 | 9.45 | + 1.0 | − 1.7 | − 0.3 |
|---|---|---|---|---|---|---|
| CAMuInc m | MC | NA | 10.76 | + 0.2 | − 1.7 | + 1.5 |
| CapApr m | LB | 4/2 | 23.68 | + 2.9 | +11.4 | +24.2 |
| EqInc m | LB | 3/3 | 20.59 | + 3.0 | + 8.4 | +16.6 |
| GovInSec m | GI | NA | 8.56 | + 1.1 | − 2.4 | + 1.6 |